# There's a Cat in Our Class!

## A Tale About Getting Along

By **Jeanie Franz Ransom**
Illustrated by **Bryan Langdo**

Magination Press • Washington, DC • American Psychological Association

Published by
MAGINATION PRESS®
An Educational Publishing Foundation Book
American Psychological Association
750 First Street NE
Washington, DC 20002

Magination Press is a registered trademark of the American Psychological Association.

For more information about our books, including a complete catalog, please write to us,
call 1-800-374-2721, or visit our website at www.apa.org/pubs/magination.

Book design by Gwen Grafft
Printed by Lake Book Manufacturing Inc., Melrose Park, IL

Library of Congress Cataloging-in-Publication Data
Names: Ransom, Jeanie Franz, 1957– author. | Langdo, Bryan, illustrator.
Title: There's a cat in our class! : a tale about getting along / by Jeanie Franz Ransom ; illustrated by Bryan Langdo.
Other titles: There is a cat in our class!
Description: Washington, DC : Magination Press, 2016. | "American Psychological Association." | Summary: When a new student, Samantha the cat, arrives, the dogs in Miss Biscuit's class learn to accept and embrace diversity.
Identifiers: LCCN 2016005288 | ISBN 9781433822629 (hardcover) | ISBN 1433822628 (hardcover)
Subjects: | CYAC: Dogs—Fiction. | Cats—Fiction. | Toleration—Fiction. | Schools—Fiction.
Classification: LCC PZ7.R1744 Th 2016 | DDC [E]—dc23 LC record available at http://lccn.loc.gov/2016005288

Manufactured in the United States of America
10 9 8 7 6 5 4 3 2 1

There were eighteen students in Miss Biscuit's class. Until…

"Criss-cross gravy sauce, paws in your lap," Miss Biscuit said as the class got in a circle for their morning meeting. "I have some exciting news! We have a new student joining us after lunch."

"A boy or a girl?" Max asked.

"A girl," Miss Biscuit said. The girls yipped and yapped.

"Not another girl," Rusty whined.

"Girls rule. Boys drool," Ginger sniffed.

"Hey, girls drool, too," Tanner said.

"Boy, girl. That doesn't matter," Miss Biscuit said. "What matters is that we make her feel welcome. I've already told Samantha that I have the nicest class in the whole school."

When the class came back
from lunch, the new student
was already there.

"Miss Biscuit, you didn't
tell us we were getting a *cat*
in our class!" Tanner said.

"I didn't think I needed to," Miss Biscuit said. "Let's show
Samantha how nice you are with a big Welcome Wag.
Give your neighbor plenty of wagging room!"

"Okay, class, it's story time," Miss Biscuit said.
"Samantha, please come join us on the rug."

Miss Biscuit's class was usually very good
about following directions. Usually.

"Tanner, what are you chewing on? Max, do you need to go to the
nurse? Ginger, leave Holly's collar alone, please. Keep your paws to
yourself! And whoever's panting, PLEASE stop," Miss Biscuit said.

"Yeah, Rusty, stop panting," Holly said.
"You're drooling all over the rug!"

"EWWWW!"

"Class!" Miss Biscuit barked. "Find a spot to sit and stay! There's plenty of room next to Samantha."

"But cats make me nervous," Rusty said.

"Me, too!" Ginger said. "I'm going to start shedding any minute!"

"I wonder how Samantha feels," Miss Biscuit said.
"She might be nervous, too. It's her first day, you know."

"But we've never had a cat in our class," Holly said.

"Maybe Samantha's never had a dog in her class,"
Miss Biscuit said. "What was your old school like, Samantha?"

"At my school, we had dogs, cats, rabbits, hamsters, even a couple of birds," Samantha said. "Sitting next to a bird was not easy, let me tell you. Especially close to lunch time." Samantha grinned. "But my best friend last year was a dog named Nutmeg. She got in trouble sometimes when she tried to herd the rabbits at recess, but we had lots of fun. And she had a gorgeous coat."

"Your coat is pretty, too," Ginger said shyly.

"Thank you," Samantha said.
"I eat lots of fish."

"Eww! Fish?" Max wrinkled his nose.
"Dogs hate fish."

Samantha smiled. "I thought so, too, until one tasted my tuna sandwich. Then, everyone begged for a bite!"

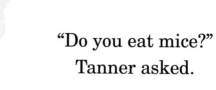

"Do you eat mice?"
Tanner asked.

"Can you walk on a leash?"
Holly wanted to know.

"Do you use a litter box or do you
go outside?" Rusty asked.

"No. Mice allergy. Yes. And yes,
I do both." Samantha said.

"Class, we have all year to
get to know each other,"
Miss Biscuit said. "Let's go to recess!"

As the students went outside, Miss Biscuit called out, "Remember, no digging, tail pulling, growling, or howling. Don't go over the fence and do stay in the yard!"

The students got busy right away picking team members
for a ball game. Soon, the only student left was Samantha.

"You take her," Max told Tanner.

"No, YOU," Tanner said.
"Cats don't know how to play fetch."

"We could teach her," Ginger said.

"Maybe tomorrow," Max said.
"There's no time today.
Recess will be over soon.
Let's play ball!"

Samantha sat and watched until...

"Somebody get the ball!
It's going to go over the fence!" Max barked.

"I'll get it!" Rusty yelped.

"I'll get it!" Holly yapped.

Everyone was tripping over their own paws trying to reach the ball. Everyone, that is, except Samantha.

With one quick movement, Samantha crossed the yard,
leaped into the air, and knocked the ball to the ground.
She pounced on it, then batted it over to her classmates.

"Wow! How'd you do that?" Max asked.
"I want *you* on my team tomorrow, Samantha!"

"I want her on *mine*!" Tanner said.

Later that day, the class was packing up to
go home when Rusty said, "Miss Biscuit,
I like having a new student in our class."

"I'm glad," Miss Biscuit said, "because we're getting another new student tomorrow."

"A cat or a dog?" Holly asked.
"A boy or a girl?" Tanner wanted to know.

"It doesn't matter, does it?" Miss Biscuit said.
"What matters is that we make our new student feel welcome."

"Let's do the Welcome Wag!" Rusty woofed.

"What about Samantha?" Max asked.
"Cats can't wag their tails."

"Or can they?" Ginger asked Samantha.